Valerie   Paul

Winnie's

Amazing Antics

Winnie's Amazing Pumpkin

Winnie in Space

Winnie Under the Sea

OXFORD
UNIVERSITY PRESS

OXFORD
UNIVERSITY PRESS

Great Clarendon Street, Oxford OX2 6DP
Oxford University Press is a department of the University of Oxford.
It furthers the University's objective of excellence in research, scholarship,
and education by publishing worldwide in
Oxford   New York

Auckland   Cape Town   Dar es Salaam   Hong Kong   Karachi
Kuala Lumpur   Madrid   Melbourne   Mexico City   Nairobi
New Delhi   Shanghai   Taipei   Toronto

With offices in

Argentina   Austria   Brazil   Chile   Czech Republic   France   Greece
Guatemala   Hungary   Italy   Japan Poland   Portugal   Singapore
South Korea   Switzerland   Thailand   Turkey   Ukraine   Vietnam

Oxford is a registered trade mark of Oxford University Press
in the UK and in certain other countries

This book first published 2014

Winnie's Amazing Pumpkin first published 2009
Winnie in Space first published 2010
Winnie Under the Sea first published 2011

The stories are complete and unabridged

2 4 6 8 10 9 7 5 3 1

British Library Cataloguing in Publication Data
Data available

ISBN: 978-0-19-273462-4

Printed in Singapore

Paper used in the production of this book is a natural,
recyclable product made from wood grown in sustainable forests.
The manufacturing process conforms to the environmental
regulations of the country of origin

Winnie's
Amazing Pumpkin

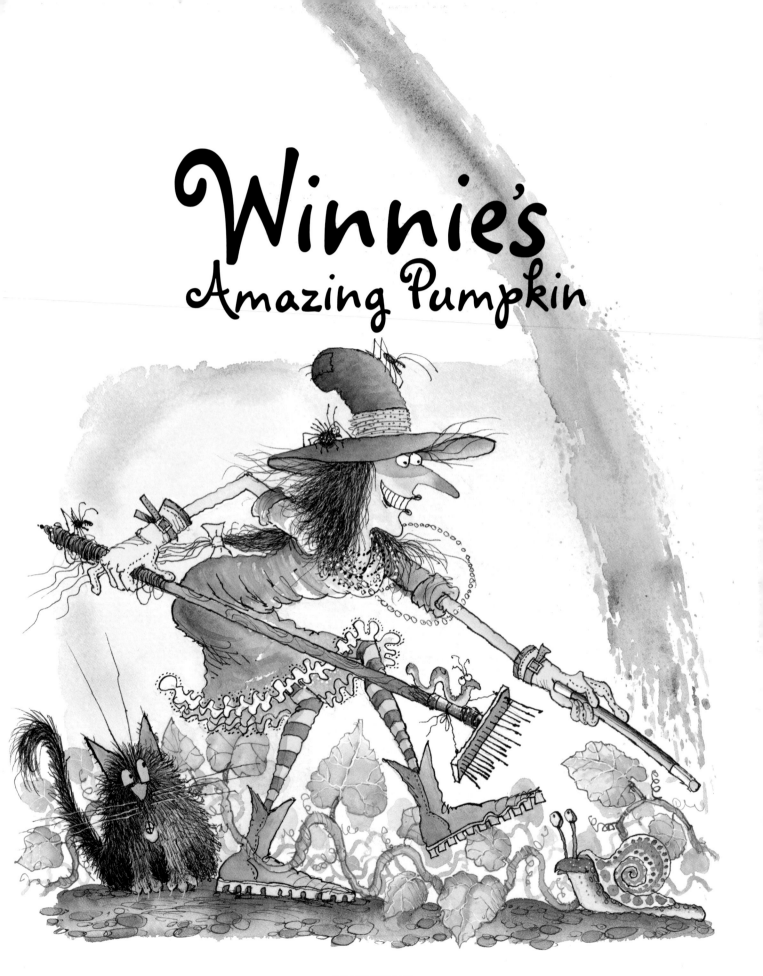

OXFORD
UNIVERSITY PRESS

Winnie the Witch ate lots of vegetables.

She liked broccoli, cauliflower,
cabbage, and parsnips.
She really liked peas, carrots,
beans, potatoes, and spinach.

But she *loved* pumpkin.
She loved pumpkin soup, pumpkin pie, and
pumpkin scones with pumpkin seeds on top.
But, most of all, she loved roast pumpkin.

Wilbur, her big black cat,
liked pumpkin soup if it
had lots of cream stirred in.

Every Saturday morning Winnie
would jump onto her broomstick,
Wilbur would jump onto her
shoulder, and they would zoom
off to the farmers' market
to buy their vegetables.

That was easy.

But it wasn't so easy coming home.
It is hard to balance on a broomstick with
a cat, pumpkins, and lots of other vegetables.

Ooops! Brussels sprouts and tomatoes
rained down on the market.

Splat! Squelch!

'Blithering broomsticks!' shouted Winnie.
And then she had a good idea.

'I'll grow my own vegetables,' she said.
So Winnie dug a big vegetable patch
in her garden.

Wilbur helped.

She planted lots and lots of vegetables.
She watered the plants and pulled up
the weeds.

Wilbur helped.

But the plants grew very slowly.

And, when they did grow, the caterpillars and snails and rabbits ate them.

'Oh dear,' said Winnie. 'Gardening is hard work. I'll try a spell to help my garden grow.'

She waved her magic wand, shouted,

Abracadabra!

and nothing happened.

'Bother!' said Winnie.
'That didn't work.
I'll go and look in my
Big Book of Spells.'

Winnie went inside
just a minute too soon.

Outside, the spell
began to work.

Inside, it was very dark.
Winnie tripped over Wilbur.

'Meooowww!'

'I'm sorry, Wilbur,' said Winnie,
'I didn't see you. It's so dark, there
must be a storm on the way.'

She looked out of the window.
It wasn't a storm.
It was Winnie's garden.
The vegetables were growing so fast
they covered all the windows.

'I'd better go out and stop
the spell,' Winnie said.

But the door wouldn't open.
An enormous cabbage was in the way.

Winnie rushed upstairs, climbed
out of the bathroom window,
and slid down a giant beanstalk.

Wilbur climbed down behind her.
This is fun! he thought,
until he met a giant caterpillar.

'Yeeoow!'

Everything in Winnie's garden was
enormous, gigantic, stupendous!

A beanstalk was growing up into the clouds.
The cabbages were as big as cows.
The rabbits were bigger than cows.
An immense pumpkin vine was curling
around Winnie's house.

And there, on the roof, was a **huge** pumpkin.
'Oh no!' shouted Winnie.
'The pumpkin will squash my house!'
She waved her magic wand,
but just as she shouted . . .

Abra . . .

CRASH!

... cadabra!

The gigantic pumpkin
crashed to the ground.

Winnie's enormous, stupendous garden
shrank back to the way it was before.

But the pumpkin that had broken
off the vine was still a massive,
monstrous, amazing pumpkin.

Winnie chopped a doorway into the pumpkin.

She made pumpkin pies, pumpkin scones, pumpkin soup with cream for Wilbur, and an enormous dish of roast pumpkin.

But there was still lots of pumpkin left.

So she put a notice on the gate:

★ FREE ★
PUMPKIN
★
Help yourself...

People came with their bowls and
baskets and even wheelbarrows.

And soon the pumpkin shell was empty.

'What shall I do with the pumpkin shell?' wondered Winnie.
'It would make a good house, but I already have a house.

One of my friends once changed a pumpkin into a coach.
But that was for a special occasion.
And the horses might be a problem.'

Then Winnie had a wonderful idea. 'Yes!' she said. 'That's exactly what it looks like,' she said. 'Of course!'

She waved her magic wand, stamped her foot, shouted,

Abracadabra!

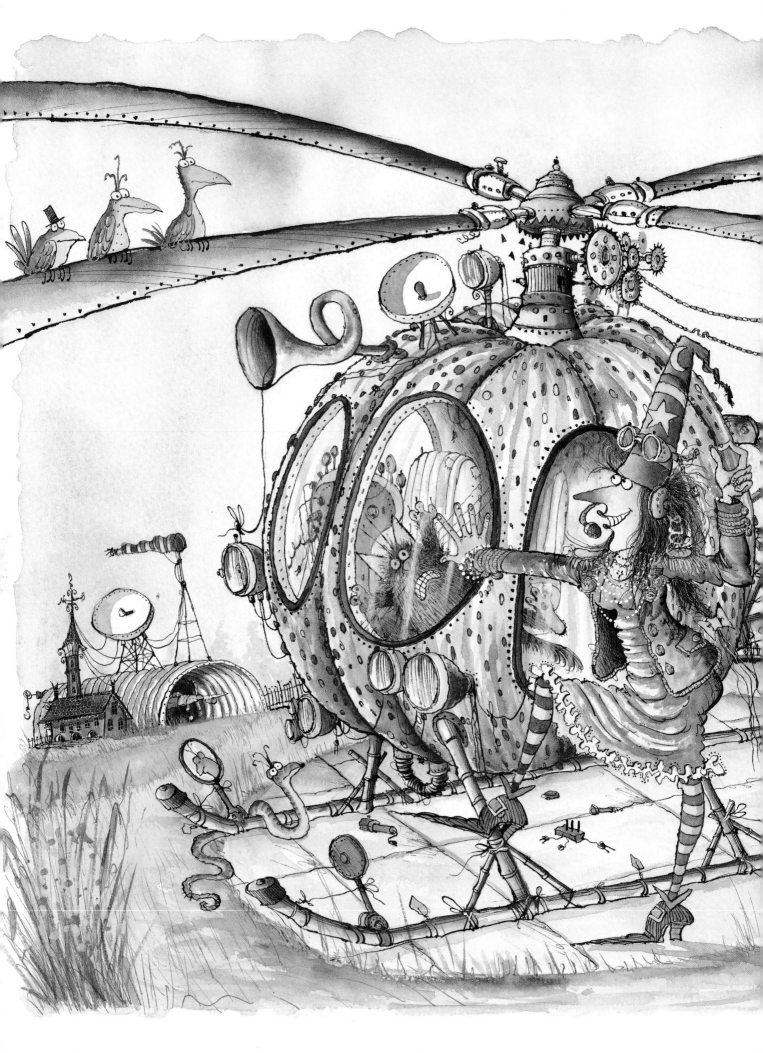

and there, in Winnie's garden,
was a bright orange helicopter.

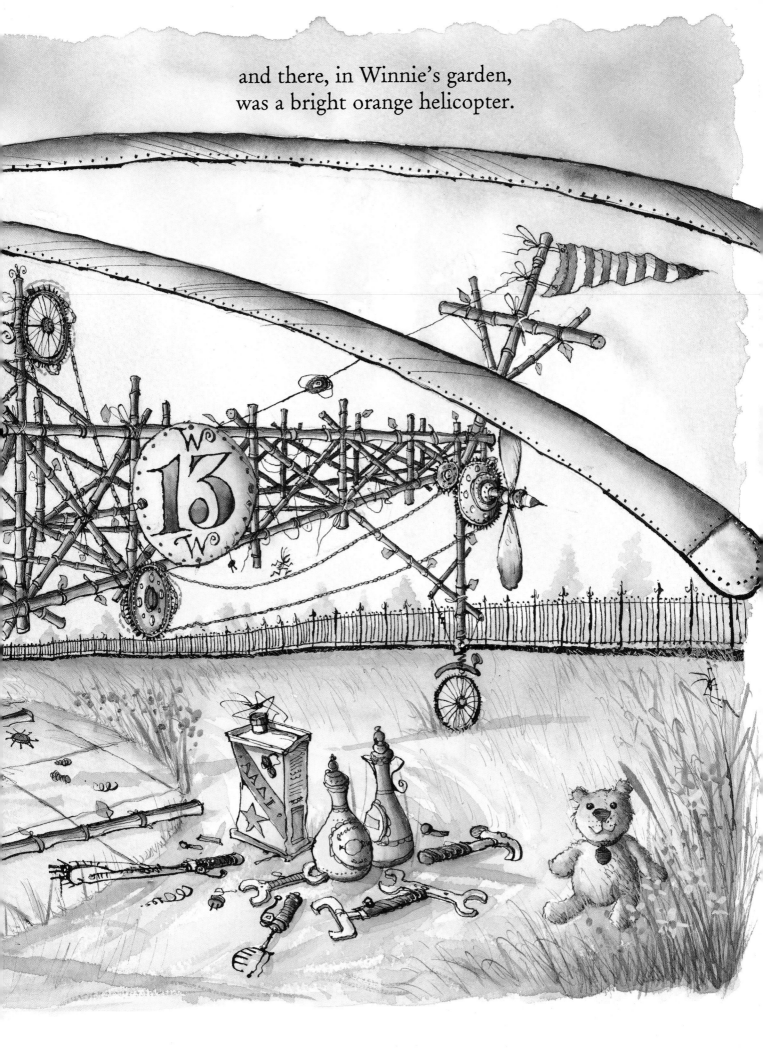

So now, when Winnie and Wilbur go to the market, Winnie can buy as many pumpkins as she likes.

And flying home in a helicopter is lots of fun!

Winnie in Space

The Sun

Winnie the Witch loved to look through her telescope at the night sky.

It was huge and dark and mysterious. 'I'd love to go into space, Wilbur,' Winnie would say. 'It would be such a big adventure.'

Wilbur, Winnie's big black cat, loved to be outside at night too. He liked to chase moths and bats and shadows.

That was enough adventure for Wilbur.

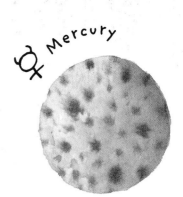

☿ Mercury

Then one night, when the Moon and stars were bright, Winnie suddenly said, 'Let's go into space right now, Wilbur!'

'Meeow?' said Wilbur.

'But how will we get there?' wondered Winnie. 'We need a rocket, and I don't have a rocket.' Then she looked up at the Moon, and she had a wonderful idea.

She waved her magic wand, shouted,

Abracadabra!

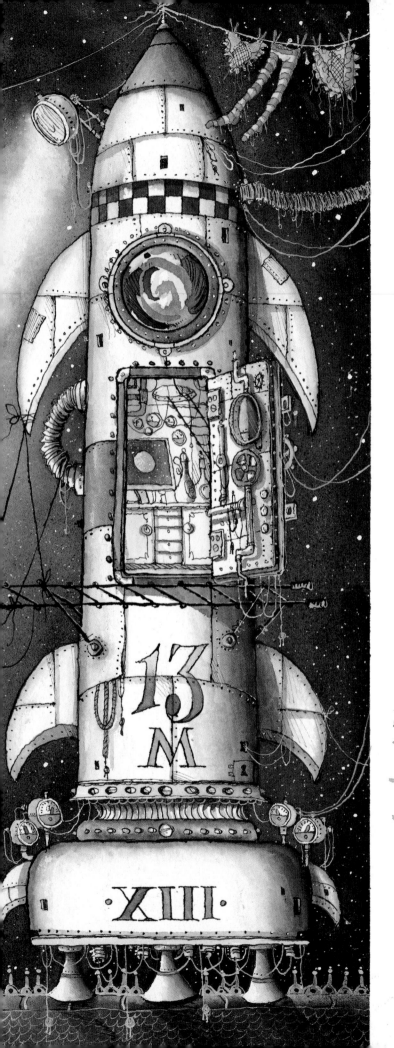

. . . and there, on the roof, was a rocket. Winnie packed a picnic basket, got her Big Book of Spells, just in case, and ran up the stairs with Wilbur.

Winnie shut her eyes, waved her magic wand, and shouted,

Abracadabra!
10 9 8 7 6 5 4 . . .

Earth

3
2
1 . . .

The rocket shot off
the roof and into space.
It went very very fast.
And it was hard to steer.

'Oops!'
Winnie nearly flew
into a satellite.

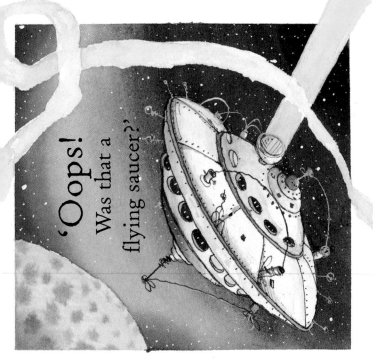

'Oops! Was that a flying saucer?'

'Oops! That was a falling star, Wilbur!'

WHOOSH!

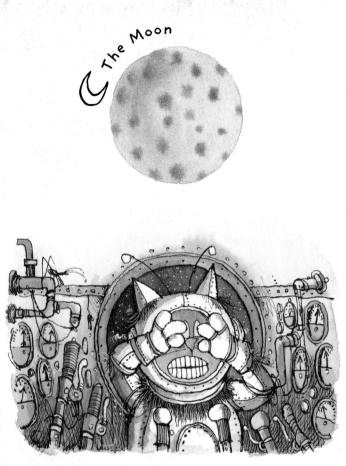

The Moon

'**Meeow!**' said Wilbur.
He put his paws over
his eyes.

'We'll find a lovely
planet for our picnic,
Wilbur,' Winnie said.

Wilbur peeped out from
behind his paws. There were
little planets everywhere.

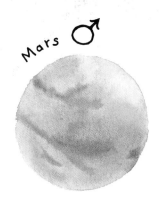

Mars ♂

'Here's a sweet little planet,' Winnie said. 'We'll have our picnic here.'

'Purr!' said Wilbur. He loved picnics.

PLOP! The rocket landed. All was quiet and peaceful. But there were funny little holes everywhere. Wilbur looked down the holes. They seemed to be empty . . .

Winnie unpacked the food. There were pumpkin scones, chocolate muffins, some cherries, and cream for Wilbur.

Yum!

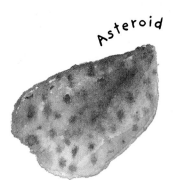

Asteroid

A little head popped out of a hole, and then there were heads everywhere.

'Rabbits!' said Winnie. 'Space rabbits are coming to our picnic!'

'**Meeow!**' said Wilbur.

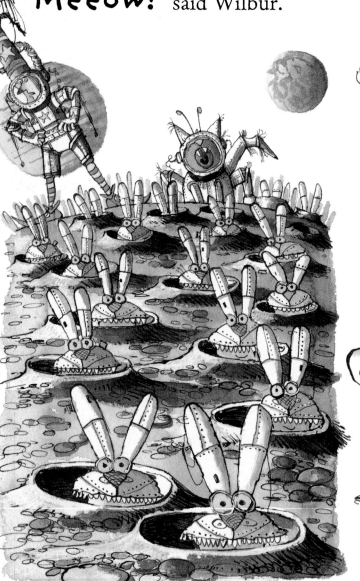

A space rabbit hopped over to try some cream. **Yuck!**

Another space rabbit tried a pumpkin scone. **Horrible.**

Chocolate muffins? **Disgusting.** Cherries? **Yuck!**

Then some of the space rabbits
hopped over to the rocket.

They sniffed it . . .

♃ Jupiter

and took a bite. Then the rocket was covered in space rabbits.

'Oh no!' shouted Winnie. She waved her magic wand, shouted,

Abracadabra!

and carrots and lettuces rained down on the rabbits. But the space rabbits didn't like carrots or lettuces.

'Of course!' said Winnie. She waved her magic wand, shouted,

Abracadabra!

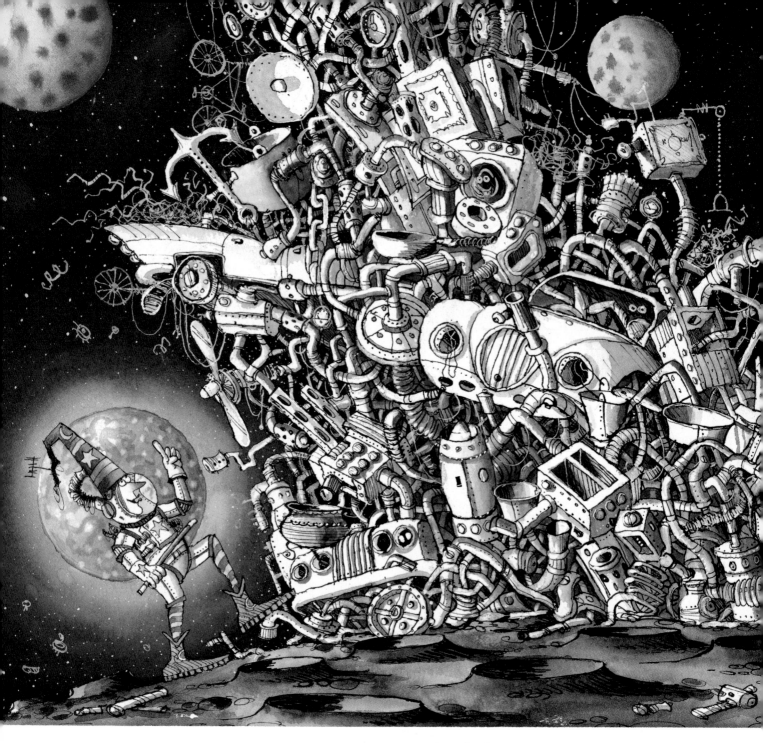

♄ Saturn

. . . and there was a giant
pile of metal.

Saucepans,
wheelbarrows,
bicycles,
cars,
even a fire engine.

Yes! That was what
space rabbits liked.

Scrumptious!

But it was too late . . .

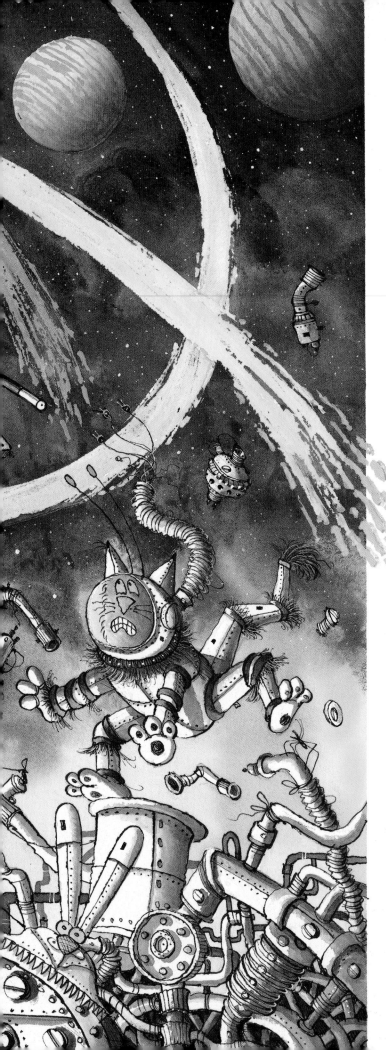

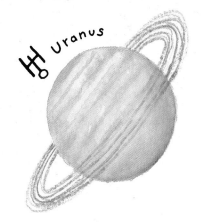
Uranus

the space rabbits had eaten up all of Winnie's metal rocket.

'Blithering broomsticks!' shouted Winnie. 'Now how will we get home?'

'**Meeeow!**' said Wilbur.

Winnie looked at the giant pile of metal. 'Perhaps,' she said. 'Maybe. I wonder.'

She looked in her Big Book of Spells. 'Yes!' she said.

Then she picked up her magic wand, waved it five times, and shouted,

Abracadabra!

There was a flash of fire, a bang . . .

Neptune

and there, on top of the giant
pile of metal, was a rattling,
roaring scrap metal rocket.

Winnie and Wilbur climbed
up to the rattling, roaring
rocket and jumped in.

VROOM!

The rocket blasted away.
It rushed and roared
through space.

Pluto

WHUMP!

The rocket landed in Winnie's garden.

'That was an adventure, Wilbur,' Winnie said. 'But I'm glad we're home.'

'Purr, purr, purr,' said Wilbur.

He was very glad to be home.

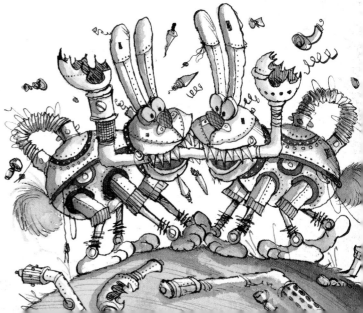

Winnie
Under the Sea

It was holiday time for Winnie the Witch and her big black cat, Wilbur.

'Where will we go this year, Wilbur?' asked Winnie. She searched the internet and found a little island, with blue sea, golden sand, and coconut trees.

The bright blue sea was full of beautiful fish.
'Don't the fish look lovely, Wilbur?' she said.
'They look delicious,' thought Wilbur.
'That's where we'll go,' said Winnie.

She packed her suitcase,
Wilbur jumped onto her shoulder,
and they zoomed up into the sky.

At last, there was the island.
It did look lovely.

They landed on the golden sand,
and found a comfortable hut.

Winnie put on her flippers and her goggles,
and dived into the water.

Wilbur climbed a coconut tree.
That was fun.
Then he had a sleep.
That was peaceful.

Winnie was having a lovely time.
The sea was full of fish.
There were dolphins,
turtles, and coral.
It was so beautiful.
Winnie wanted Wilbur
to see it, too.

'Wilbur,' called Winnie,
'come and see the fish.
You'll love them!'

Wilbur wanted to see the fish.
He put one paw in the water.
Erk! Nasty! It was wet!
'Meeeeoooow!' cried Wilbur.
He hated getting wet.

GHOTI

Then Winnie had
a wonderful idea.
She waved her
magic wand, shouted,

Abracadabra!

and Wilbur was
no longer a cat.

He was a cat-fish!

Wilbur the cat-fish dived
into the waves and swam away.

Winnie watched him through her goggles.

He chased some tiny fish.
Then he dived under a dogfish
and played catch with a crayfish.

Wilbur the cat-fish was having so much fun,
Winnie wanted to be a fish as well.

But she couldn't be a fish.
She had to hold her magic wand.
What could she be?
Of course!

Winnie waved her wand, shouted,

Abracadabra!

and she was an octopus!
An octopus with orange
and yellow legs, holding
a magic wand!

It was fun being an octopus.
Winnie the octopus waved her eight legs
and floated through the seaweed,
around the coral, over the rocks.

Wilbur the cat-fish darted around her.
Thousands of fish swam with them.
Tiny fish, big fish, and, suddenly . . .

a sea lion.

The sea lion flipped its tail,
and Winnie lost her wand.

She grabbed at it, but missed.

A swordfish tried to spear it for her, but missed.

A jellyfish nearly caught it, but missed.

Down, down it sank,

into the wreck of
an old sailing ship,

and disappeared.

'Blithering broomsticks!' wailed Winnie,
but it sounded like, 'Bubble, bubble, bubble.'
'Bubble, bubble, bubble,' cried Wilbur.

They didn't want to stay under the sea for ever.
Where was the magic wand?
Stuck in the anchor? **No.**

Under the ropes? **No.**   Behind the big crab? **No.**

Wilbur flipped it out.
Winnie grabbed it,
waved it five times,
shouted,

Abracadabra!

In the treasure chest? **Yes!**

and a **witch** and a **cat** floated back to the shore.

'That was exciting, Wilbur,' Winnie said.
'Too exciting. We won't do that again.
But it is beautiful under the sea.'

Then Winnie had another wonderful idea.

A little yellow boat was bobbing on the waves.
Winnie waved her magic wand, shouted,

GHOTI

Abracadabra!

and there, bobbing on the waves . . .

was a yellow submarine.

Winnie and Wilbur went on board.
The fish swam up to the windows and looked in.

'It is lovely under the sea, isn't it Wilbur,' said Winnie.
'It's lovely and dry in here,' Wilbur thought.
'Purr, purr, purr,' he said.